MW01107401

Andrew is worried about who he will play with, where he will eat lunch, and if his teacher will be kind.

He asked his parents many
questions about school.

His parents said "Don't worry Andrew. It will be okay."

But Andrew wasn't so sure.

Andrew's knees were trembling, his hooves were sweaty, his heart was racing,

and there were butterflies in his belly.

Andrew wasn't sure what to do so he went to visit his favorite forest.

On his way, the wind whispered to him "Smell the sunflowers. Blow out the birthday candles."

That's odd, Andrew thought.

But he tried it anyways

breathing in... and out.

Andrew went and sat beside a tree. He imagined he had beautiful roots that went deep into the earth,

just like the tree.

Then, Andrew got very still. He noticed all the sensations around him and inside him. He noticed the birds singing, butterflies flying past him, the ground under him, and the smell of late summer air.

He felt very peaceful.

But the next morning, Andrew
woke up very anxious about school.

"Oh no," Andrew thought.

Andrew walked very quietly to school with his dad.

The school building looked so big and scary to Andrew.

Andrew took off his backpack and looked around.

He was very nervous, but he remembered what he learned under the tree.

Andrew had noticed a friend to play with. He walked over and said hello. His new friend's name was Berry.

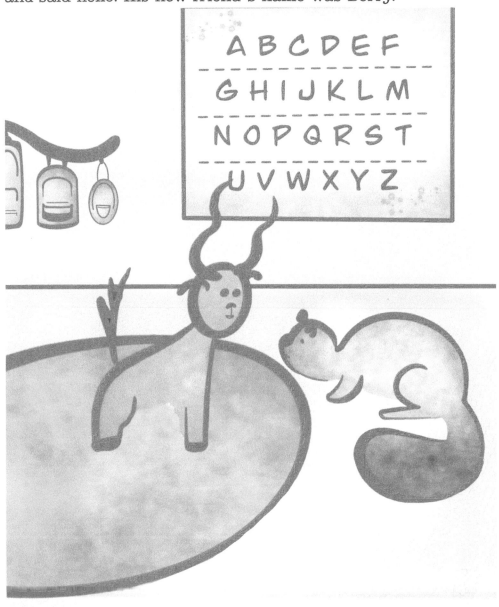

Berry and Andrew had a wonderful time playing games together.

At lunch time, Andrew was not sure where to sit.

He remembered what the wind said to him.

Andrew found a place to sit next to a new classmate named Danny. They ate their lunch together and talked about how much they loved splashing in the river.

Andrew played games all afternoon with his new friends.

On the way out the door, Andrew's teacher said "I loved how you introduced yourself to new friends Andrew. Great job!"

Andrew's dad asked him how school was.

"It was amazing," he said.

Questions For Kids

Why do you think we feel anxious sometimes? How do you think this feeling helps us? What kinds of things do you notice in your body when you feel anxious? What kinds of actions do you do when you feel anxious like Andrew did? Do you think Andrew's parents were being mean when they told him not to worry? Do you think Andrew's friends might also be feeling anxious? What kinds of situations make you feel anxious? How do you like to feel calmer and trust that things are going to be okay?

Considerations For The Bigger Kids And The Kids At Heart

Just like how we generally feel physical pain when something is wrong in our bodies, I think we generally feel emotional pain when something is not right in our emotional bodies. Anxiety is a challenging emotion that still carries cultural shame, just like any 'negative' emotion. Nevertheless, there is no shame in a twisted ankle, and so I believe there should be no shame in feeling anxious. <u>Anxiety is an indicator emotion letting one know that something is not fully calibrating.</u> Just like how a check engine light in a car can tell us valuable information, so too will our emotions when we know how to recognize them, acknowledge them and move through them.

However, we are often told to calm down, get over it, or just be happy all the time. Consequently, we just may forget the small warning signs of anxiety. Perhaps we begin to numb our emotions until we are in the midst of intense and possibly debilitating feelings. Numbing – when we choose to turn off our feelings – can lead to addictive behaviors and overindulgences in all forms to mask the pain of something wrong. <u>Instead, why not recognize the feeling, take a few deep breaths, and honor the important information being given to us by our bodies and minds.</u> This may lead us to the deeper causes of the issue instead of using numbing as a superficial response. When we acknowledge our feelings, we have the space to think more clearly about our situations and choose the highest path available.

For more resources check out www.BetterHelp.com www.YourLifeCounts.com or www.TalkSpace.com